THIS BLOOMSBURY BOOK

BELONGS TO

....

For Milo, from Oupa, with love – *L.B.*

For Catherine and Simon – *S.H.*

First published in Great Britain in 2006 by Bloomsbury Publishing Plc
36 Soho Square, London, W1D 3QY

This paperback edition first published in 2007

Text copyright © Louis Baum 2006
Illustrations copyright © Sue Hellard 2006

A CIP catalogue record of this book is available from the British Library

ISBN 978 0 7475 8402 5

Printed by Tien Wah Press in Singapore

10 9 8 7 6 5 4 3 2 1

All papers used by Bloomsbury Publishing are natural, recyclable products
made from wood grown in well-managed forests. The manufacturing processes
conform to the environmental regulations of the country of origin.

Milo Mouse
and the Scary Monster

Louis Baum

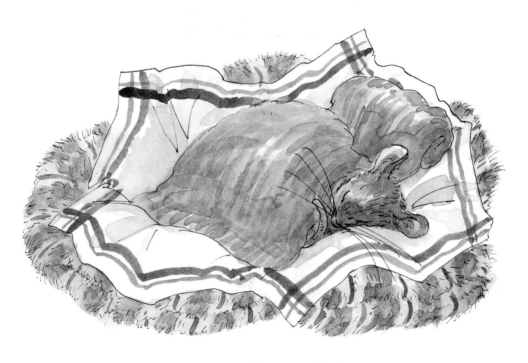

Illustrated by Sue Hellard

BLOOMSBURY
CHILDREN'S
BOOKS

When Milo Mouse woke up in the morning he felt awful.

'Mum,' he said, 'I had a bad dream last night. I was frightened.'

'Well, maybe it would help if you told me what it was about,' said Mum.

Milo Mouse shivered. 'It was night-time and dark and there was a horrible big scary monster running after me. I didn't really get to see the monster, but I knew it had huge horrible claws.'

'Oh my,' said Mum. 'That does sound horrible!'
Mum thought for a moment and said, 'I should
think a lovely cup of warm milk just before
bedtime will make sure you don't have that
horrible dream again.'

So, that night, that's what Milo Mouse had.
A lovely cup of warm milk just before bedtime.

Then Milo Mouse crept past the dark cupboard
under the stairs. And, heart beating fast, he
rushed upstairs to bed.

When Milo Mouse woke up the next morning he felt even more awful.

'Dad, I had a bad dream last night,' said Milo Mouse.

'Well, maybe it would help if you told me what it was about,' said Dad.

Milo Mouse shivered. 'It was night-time and dark and there was a horrible big scary monster just behind me, trying to catch me. I didn't really get to see the monster, but the faster I ran the bigger it got. And I didn't really see, but I just knew that it had huge horrible fangs.'

'Oh my,' said Dad. 'That doesn't sound very enjoyable at all!'
Dad thought for a moment and said, 'They do say that keeping
a window open to let in the fresh night air works wonders.'
So, that night, that's what Milo Mouse did.

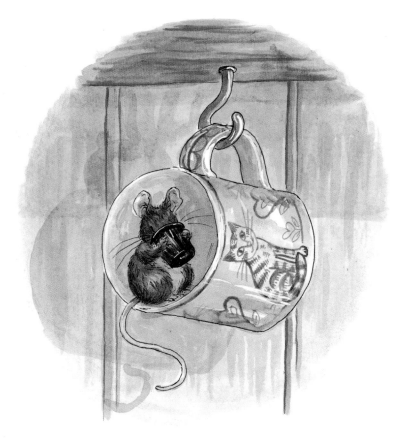

He had a lovely cup of warm milk just before bedtime.

Then Milo Mouse crept past the dark cupboard under the stairs.

And, heart beating fast, he rushed
upstairs to bed, opened the
window and let in the fresh
night air.

When Milo Mouse woke up the next morning he felt
even worse than the day before.

He went straight to his big brother Jack.

'Jack,' he said, 'I had
a bad dream last night.'
'Well, maybe it would help if you
told me what it was about,' said Jack.

Milo Mouse shivered.

'It was night-time and dark and horrible and there was a big scary monster trying to catch me. I couldn't really see it, but I knew that if it caught me it would do horrible things to me. The faster I ran the bigger the monster got. And I didn't really see, but I knew it had horrible scary big glinting eyes.'

'Oh my,' said Jack. 'That does sound pretty horrible!'

'It was,' said Milo.

Jack thought for a moment. Then he said, 'Try some exercise, Milo. I used to have bad dreams and I exercised before bedtime and it really worked.'

So, that night, that's what Milo Mouse did.
First he had a lovely cup of warm milk.

Then he crept past the dark cupboard
under the stairs and, heart beating
fast, he rushed upstairs to bed.

He opened the window to let
in the fresh night air, and
then he did twelve exercises.

When Milo Mouse woke up the next morning he felt the most awful he'd ever felt. And he felt awful all day. Because now he had no one else to ask for help.

Before he went to bed that night he had a lovely cup of warm milk. Then, heart beating fast, he crept past the dark cupboard under the stairs. But, instead of rushing upstairs, he stopped and turned. The door was open and now there was a light on. 'I wonder what's inside that cupboard,' thought Milo Mouse. Trembling all over, he peeped around the door.

Inside the cupboard were sheets,
pillowcases and some big fluffy bath towels.
'Oh,' said Milo Mouse, still trembling a bit.
'Sheets and towels are nothing to be afraid of.'

Then Milo Mouse went upstairs and left the window open really wide to let in the fresh night air.

And that night he did fifteen exercises.

When he got into bed he lay awake a long, long time.
The last thing he wanted was to fall asleep and meet
that horrible scary monster again.

Milo Mouse thought about the monster

and its claws

and its fangs.

He thought about the monster's horrible scary big glinting eyes.
He thought about the monster's horrible growls getting louder and louder.

Then he thought about the dark cupboard under the stairs.
And how tonight he'd looked in.
And how inside the cupboard there were sheets,
pillowcases and big fluffy bath towels.

And as he fell asleep, Milo Mouse had a smile on his face.

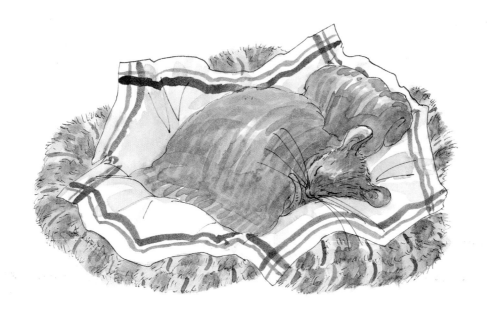

But in Milo Mouse's dream it was night-time and dark, and horrible and scary. Milo Mouse ran as fast as he could, but something was running behind him. And the faster Milo Mouse ran, the faster the thing behind him ran.

Milo Mouse's heart beat fast, he tried to run faster but he was getting out of breath. His little paws felt heavy, and he felt very tired, and he knew that whatever was behind him was quickly catching up.

But then Milo
Mouse remembered
the dark cupboard
under the stairs
filled with sheets,
pillowcases and big
fluffy bath towels.

Milo Mouse
stopped.

The thing behind
him stopped.

Milo Mouse
turned around.

Suddenly he woke up and sitting beside him on his bed was a dormouse, half the size of Milo Mouse.

'Who are you?' demanded Milo Mouse.

'I'm Logan Dormouse,' said the dormouse. 'I sleep in that little jewellery box on the windowsill, and every night I've been trying to wake you up to play.'

'I thought you were a horrible scary monster,' said Milo Mouse.

'Me, a horrible scary monster?' said Logan Dormouse. 'Don't make me laugh.' And he laughed.

Milo Mouse laughed too.

'Can we be friends?' Logan Dormouse asked.

Milo Mouse thought for a minute. 'That sounds like a good idea,' said Milo Mouse. 'Yes. Let's be friends.'

So they were.

And they played lots of games together. But the game they liked playing most was …

scary
monsters!

Enjoy more fantastic picture books from Bloomsbury Children's Books . . .

Princesses Are Not Quitters!
by Kate Lum
& Sue Hellard

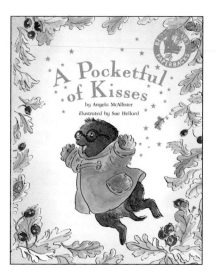

A Pocketful of Kisses
by Angela McAllister
& Sue Hellard

Tea with Bea
by Louis Baum
& Georgie Birkett

The 108th Sheep
by Ayano Imai